First published in Great Britain 2003
By Egmont Books Limited
239 Kensington High Street, London W8 6SA
Illustrated by Andrew Grey
Based on the 'Winnie-the-Pooh' works
By A.A. Milne and E.H. Shepard
© 2003 Disney Enterprises, Inc.
Designed by Clare Doughty
Edited by Catherine Shoolbred
Design © 2003 Egmont Books Limited
All Rights Reserved.

1 3 5 7 9 10 8 6 4 2

ISBN 1 4052 0528 8

Printed in Singapore.

Piglet Has A Bath

Nobody seemed to know where they came from, but there they were in the Forest: Kanga and Baby Roo. Pooh asked Christopher Robin, "How did they come here?" Christopher Robin said, "In the Usual Way, if you know what I mean, Pooh."

And Pooh said, "Ah!" Then he went to call upon Piglet to see what he thought and at Piglet's house he found Rabbit, so they all talked about it.

"What I don't like about it is this," said Rabbit. "Here are we, all of us, and then suddenly, we wake up one morning, and what do we find? We find a Strange animal among us. An animal who carries her family about with her in her pocket!"

"The question is," said Piglet, "what are we to do about Kanga?"

"The best way," said Rabbit, "would be this. Hide Baby Roo and then when Kanga says, 'Where's Baby Roo?' we say, 'Aha!'"

"Aha!" said Pooh, practising.

"We say 'Aha!'" said Rabbit, "so Kanga knows that we know where Baby Roo is. 'Aha!' means 'We'll tell you where Roo is, if you promise to go away and never come back to the Forest.'"

"There's just one thing," said Piglet, fidgeting a bit. "Christopher Robin said a Kanga was Generally Regarded as One of the Fiercer Animals. And it is well known that if One of the Fiercer Animals is Deprived of Its Young, it becomes as fierce as Two of the Fiercer Animals. In which case 'Aha!' is perhaps a foolish thing to say!"

"Piglet," said Rabbit, "you haven't any pluck."

"It is hard to be brave," said Piglet, sniffing slightly, "when you're only a Very Small Animal."

Rabbit, who had begun to write very busily, looked up and said: "It is because you are a Very Small Animal that you will be Useful in the adventure before us."

Piglet was so excited at the idea of being Useful that he forgot to be frightened.

"What about me?" said Pooh sadly. "I suppose I shan't be useful?"

"Never mind, Pooh," said Piglet comfortingly.

"Without Pooh," said Rabbit solemnly, "the adventure would be impossible."

"Oh!" said Piglet, and tried not to look disappointed. Pooh went into a corner of the room and said proudly to himself, "Impossible without Me! That sort of Bear."

"Now listen all of you," said Rabbit, when he had finished writing, and Pooh and Piglet sat listening very eagerly.

This was what Rabbit read out:

PLAN tO CAPTURE BABY ROO

1   General Remarks. Kanga runs faster than any of Us, even Me.

2. More General Remarks. Kanga never takes her eye off Baby Roo, except when he's safely buttoned up in her pocket.

3   Therefore. If we are to Capture Baby Roo, we must get a Long Start, because Kanga runs faster than any of Us, even Me. (See 1.)

4   A Thought. If Roo had jumped out of Kanga's pocket and Piglet had jumped in, Kanga wouldn't know the difference, because Piglet is a very Small Animal.

5   Like Roo.

6   But Kanga would have to be looking the other way first, so as not to see Piglet jumping in.

7   See 2

8   Another Thought. But if Pooh was talking to her very excitedly, she might look the other way for a moment.

9   And then I could run away with Roo.

10 Quickly.

11 And Kanga wouldn't discover the difference until Afterwards.

Rabbit

For a little while nobody said anything. And then
Piglet said: "And - Afterwards? When Kanga does
Discover the Difference?"

"Then we all say 'Aha!' Why, what's the trouble,
Piglet?" said Rabbit.

"Nothing," said Piglet, "as long as we all three
say it. I shouldn't care to say 'Aha!' by myself.
It wouldn't sound nearly so well."

"Well, Pooh?" said Rabbit. "You see what *you*
have to do?"

"No," said Pooh Bear. "Not yet," he said.
"What do I do?"

"You just have to talk **very hard** to Kanga so as she doesn't notice anything."

"Oh! What about?"

"Anything you like."

"You mean like telling her a little bit of poetry or something?"

"That's it," said Rabbit. "Splendid. Now come along."

So they all went out to look for Kanga.

Kanga and Roo were in a sandy part of the Forest. Baby Roo was practising very small jumps in the sand, and falling down mouse-holes and climbing out of them. Kanga was saying, "Just one more jump, dear, and then we must go home."

And at that moment who should come stumping up the hill, but Pooh.

"Good afternoon, Kanga."

"Good afternoon, Pooh."

"We were just going home," said Kanga. "Good afternoon, Rabbit. Good afternoon, Piglet."

Rabbit and Piglet, who had come up from the other side of the hill, said "Good afternoon," and Roo asked them to look at him jumping, so they stayed and looked.

"Oh, Kanga," said Pooh, after Rabbit had winked at him twice, "I don't know if you are interested in Poetry at all?"

"Hardly at all," said Kanga.

"Oh!" said Pooh.

"Go on," said Rabbit, in a loud whisper behind his paw.
"Talking of Poetry," said Pooh, "I made up a little piece
as I was coming along. It went like this. Er – now let
me see –"
"You must listen very carefully," said Rabbit to Kanga.
"So as not to miss any of it," said Piglet.
"Oh, yes," said Kanga, but she still looked at Baby Roo.

Pooh gave a little cough and began.

LINES WRITTEN BY
A BEAR OF VERY LITTLE BRAIN

On Monday, when the sun is hot
I wonder to myself a lot:
"Now is it true, or is it not,
"That what is which and which is what?"

On Tuesday, when it hails and snows,
The feeling on me grows and grows
That hardly anybody knows
If those are these or these are those.

On Wednesday, when the sky is blue,
And I have nothing else to do,
I sometimes wonder if it's true
That who is what and what is who.

On Thursday, when it starts to freeze
And hoar-frost twinkles on the trees,
How very readily one sees
That these are whose - but whose are these?

On Friday -

"Yes, it is, isn't it?" said Kanga, not waiting to hear what happened on Friday.

"Just one more jump, Roo, dear, and then we really must be going."

"Talking of Poetry," said Pooh quickly, "have you ever noticed that tree right over there?"

"No," said Kanga. "Jump in, Roo, dear, and we'll go home."

"You ought to look at that tree right over there," said Rabbit. "Shall I lift you in, Roo?" And he picked up Roo in his paws.

"I can see a bird in it from here," said Pooh. "Or is it a fish?"

"It isn't a fish, it's a bird," said Piglet.

"So it is," said Rabbit.

And then at last Kanga did turn her head to look. And the moment that her head was turned, Rabbit said in a loud voice "In you go, Roo!" and in jumped Piglet into Kanga's pocket, and off scampered Rabbit, with Roo in his paws, as fast as he could.

"Are you all right, Roo, dear?" said Kanga.

Piglet made a squeaky Roo-noise from the bottom of Kanga's pocket.

"Rabbit had to go away," said Pooh. "I think he thought of something he had to go and see about **suddenly**."

"And Piglet?"

"I think Piglet thought of something at the same time. **Suddenly**."

"Well, we must be getting home," said Kanga. "Goodbye, Pooh."

And in **three large jumps** she was gone.

Pooh looked after her as she went.

"I wish I could jump like that," he thought. "Some can and some can't. That's how it is."

But there were moments when Piglet wished that Kanga couldn't. Often, when he had had a long walk home through the Forest, he had wished that he were a bird; but now he thought jerkily to himself at the bottom of Kanga's pocket, "If this is flying I shall never really take to it."

And he was saying,

all the way to Kanga's house.

Of course as soon as Kanga unbuttoned her pocket, she saw what had happened. For a moment she was **frightened**, and then she knew she wasn't; for she felt sure that Christopher Robin would never let any harm happen to Roo. So she said to herself, "If they are having a joke with me, I will have a joke with them."

"Now then, Roo, dear," she said, as she took Piglet out of her pocket. "Bedtime."

"Aha!" said Piglet, as well as he could after his **Terrifying Journey**. But it wasn't a very good "Aha!" and Kanga didn't seem to understand what it meant.

"Bath first," said Kanga in a cheerful voice. Piglet looked round for the others. But the others weren't there!

Rabbit was playing with Baby Roo in his own house, and feeling more **fond** of him every minute,

and Pooh, who had decided to be a Kanga, was **still** at the sandy place at the top of the Forest, practising jumps.

"I wonder," said Kanga, "if it would be a good idea
to have a **cold bath** this evening. Would you like
that, Roo, dear?"

Piglet had never been really fond of baths, so in as
brave a voice as he could he said:

"Kanga, I am not Roo, I am Piglet!"

"Yes, dear, yes," said Kanga, soothingly. "And imitating
Piglet's voice too! So clever of him," she went on, as
she took a large bar of soap out of the cupboard.

"Can't you see?" shouted Piglet. "Haven't you got eyes?
Look at me!"

"I am looking, Roo, dear," said Kanga rather severely.
"And if you go on making faces like Piglet's, you will
grow up to look like Piglet – and then think how
sorry you will be. Now then, into the bath, and don't
let me have to speak to you about it again."

Before he knew where he was, Piglet was in the bath,
and Kanga was scrubbing him firmly with a
large lathery flannel.

"Ow!" cried Piglet. "Let me out! I'm Piglet!"

"Don't open the mouth, dear, or the soap goes in,"
said Kanga. "There! What did I tell you?"

"You – you – you did it on purpose," spluttered Piglet,
as soon as he could speak again.

"That's right, dear, don't say anything," said Kanga,
and in another minute Piglet was out of the bath,
and being rubbed dry with a towel.

"Now," said Kanga, "there's your medicine, and then bed."
"W-w-what medicine?" said Piglet.
"To make you grow big and strong, dear. You don't want to grow up small and weak like Piglet, do you? Well, then!"
At that moment there was a knock at the door.
"Come in," said Kanga, and in came Christopher Robin.

"Christopher Robin!" cried Piglet. "Tell Kanga who
I am! She keeps saying I'm Roo. I'm not Roo, am I?"
Christopher Robin looked at him very carefully,
and shook his head.

"You can't be Roo," he said, "because I've just seen
Roo playing in Rabbit's house."

"There you are!" said Piglet. "I told you so. I'm Piglet."
Christopher Robin shook his head again.

"Oh, you're not Piglet," he said. "I know Piglet
well, and he's quite a different colour."

Piglet began to say that this was because he had just
had a bath, and as he opened his mouth, Kanga slipped
the medicine spoon in and patted him on the back.

"I knew it wasn't Piglet," said Kanga. "I wonder who it can be?"

"Perhaps it's some relation of Pooh's," said Christopher Robin.

Kanga agreed this was probably what it was, and said that they would have to call it by some name.

"I shall call it Pootel," said Christopher Robin. "Henry Pootel for short."

And just when this was decided, Henry Pootel wriggled out of Kanga's arms and ran to the open door. Never had Henry Pootel Piglet run so fast as he ran then. He didn't stop running until he had got quite close to his house. But when he was a hundred yards away, he stopped running and

rolled

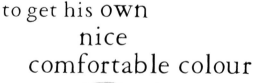

the rest

of the way home,

to get his own

nice

comfortable colour

again.

So Kanga and Roo stayed in the Forest. And every Tuesday Roo spent the day with his great friend Rabbit, and every Tuesday Kanga spent the day teaching her great friend Pooh to jump, and every Tuesday Piglet spent the day with his great friend Christopher Robin. So they were all happy again.

THIS StoRY TOOK PLACE